Pip and Pop

Written by Natasha Paul

Illustrated by Erin Brown

Collins

Kim picks the kit.

Pip tips the sack.

Pip can pat it.

Pop can tap it.

Kim pops it in.

Kim pops the cap.

Pop can dip it.

Pip pops the cap.

It is on the cat!

Pop packs the sack.

Pip picks a man.

13

/k/

14

ck

After reading

Letters and Sounds: Phase 2

Word count: 50

Focus phonemes: /o/ /c/ /k/ ck

Common exception words: the, is

Curriculum links: Expressive arts and design

Early learning goals: Reading: read and understand simple sentences; use phonic knowledge to decode regular words and read them aloud accurately; read some common irregular words

Developing fluency

- Your child may enjoy hearing you read the book.
- Take turns to read a page. Encourage your child to read with expression, and use a tone to mimic the sounds of the words **tick tock** (page 7) and **POP** (page 10).

Phonic practice

- Remind your child that two letters can make one sound. On page 2, point to **picks** and ask your child to sound and blend the word (*p/i/ck/s*). Ask: Which two letters make the /k/ sound? (*ck*) Can they find the same sound but spelt differently on this page? (*K/i/m, k/i/t*)
- On page 4, ask them to find the /k/ sound. How is it spelt? (*c/a/n, c*)
- Look at the "I spy sounds" pages (14–15). Point to the kettle on page 14 and then the /k/ at the top of the page and say: I spy a /k/ in kettle. Challenge your child to point to and name different things they can see containing the /k/ or ck sound. (e.g. *sink, fork, cutlery, cake, case, curtain, cucumber, cupboard, sock, duck, building blocks, socket*) You could ask your child about spellings, e.g. Ask: How is the /k/ in that word spelt?

Extending vocabulary

- Turn to page 10. Discuss the meaning of **pops** and how it makes the sound of a pop. Turn to page 7 and discuss how **tick tock** sounds like a clock.
- Ask your child if they can think of other words that sound like their meaning. (e.g. *bang, thump, ting, bong*)